BROCCOLI'S BIG DAY!

Mike Henson
Sandra de la Prada

 happy yak

One day, Broccoli heard a **click, click, pop** at her door.

An official-looking envelope had swished through her letterbox and landed on the doormat.

Inside was an invitation from the Annual Vegetable Awards selection committee.

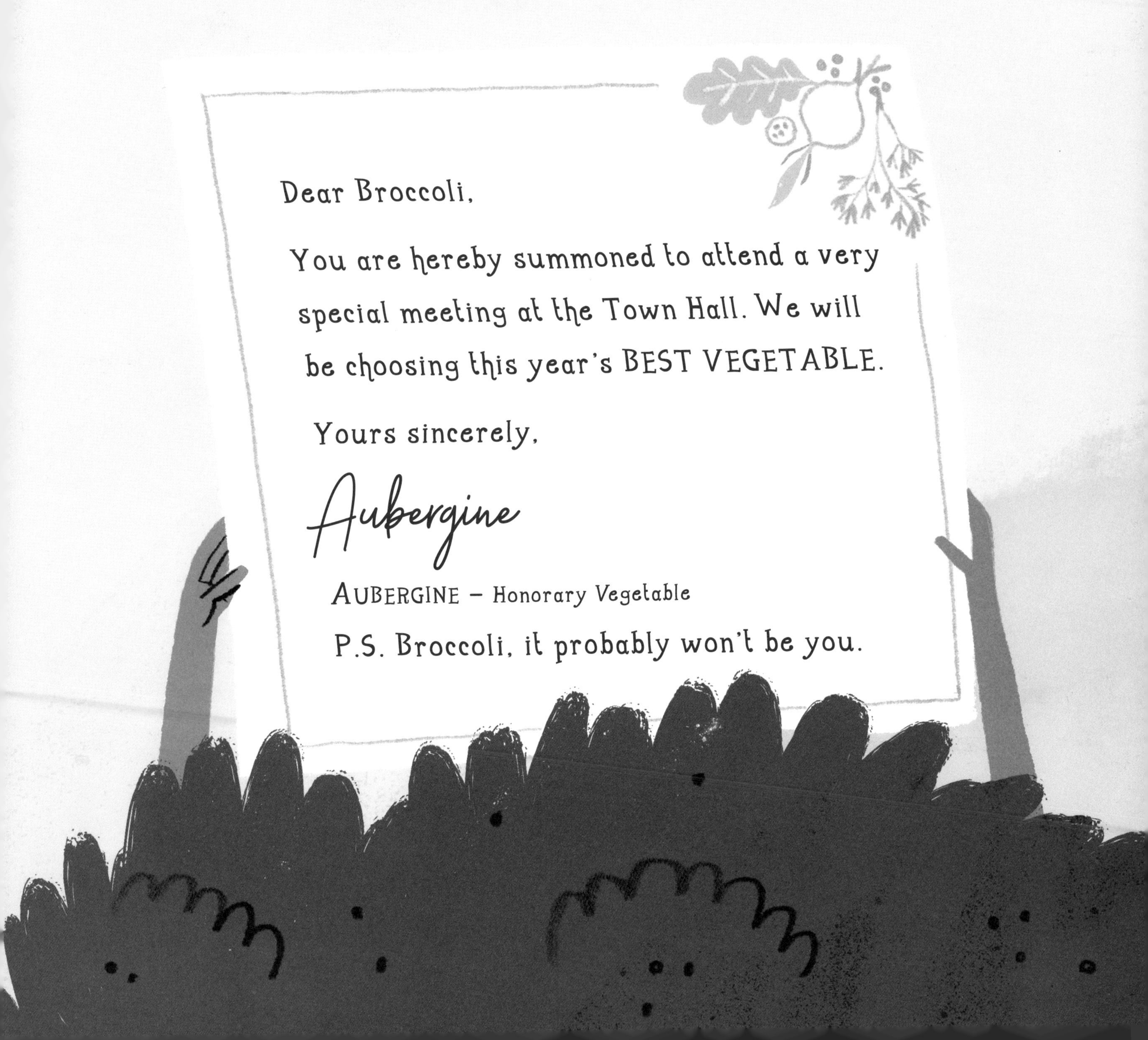
Dear Broccoli,

You are hereby summoned to attend a very special meeting at the Town Hall. We will be choosing this year's BEST VEGETABLE.

Yours sincerely,

Aubergine

AUBERGINE – Honorary Vegetable

P.S. Broccoli, it probably won't be you.

"Oh no," sighed Broccoli.
"It probably *won't* be me!
I haven't done *anything*
special this year."

But Broccoli knew that her best
friend Carrot would be at the
meeting, so she decided to go.

The journey into town was all very normal. Broccoli jumped onto her bike and skilfully swerved and skidded down Vege-Table Mountain.

It was always super-slippery, but Broccoli loved living in a house with a view, so she didn't really mind the slope.

Then she had to fight off the grouchy bees that chased her around Super Stinky Swamp, but that was all pretty normal too.

Mrs Plum's cat was stuck up one of the celery trees again, so Broccoli stopped to make a speedy rescue.

That was also **very normal**.

In no time at all, Broccoli was approaching the Town Hall. She whizzed past some cyclists as she zoomed round the last corner.

"Oh, maybe those cyclists are having a
who-can-race-the-slowest race," thought Broccoli.

Broccoli arrived and quietly joined the other guests, who were all waiting for Aubergine to start.

“Vegetation,” began Aubergine. “We are hereby gathered to choose this year’s Best Vegetable. All participating guests must therefore take it in turns to explain why *they* think they should win this year’s award.”

Broccoli was very pleased to be sitting next to Carrot. Leaning over, she whispered, "Carrot, why does Aubergine always use such ludicrously long words?"

Carrot shrugged.
"Because she's fancy?"

"Ahh, Carrot," said Aubergine,

"I see you are volunteering to go first!

So,

why do you think

YOU

are the Best Vegetable?"

Carrot went a funny reddish-orange colour.
"I am the best," said Carrot, "because of
my amazing hair."

"*And* because I went diving to the deep, dark bottom of the sea."

Broccoli wasn't so sure this bit was true, but she kept quiet and listened to what the other vegetables had to say.

"Rubbish!" scoffed Rocket Leaf.
"That's nothing special. I flew to the moon and back in my... um... er... rocket.

I'm a super leaf – in fact I'm out of this world! And that is why I nominate myself to be this year's Best Vegetable."

“Who’s the best? That’s easy peasy!” chorused the Pea Pod Posse. “We stuck together and went skiing through the Wobbly Wild Woods, home of the white, whistling wolves. And these wolves are VEGETARIAN…”

"Only Pedro got a
little bit squished!"

“Easy peasy, indeed!” said Tomato.
“Well, I went trekking through the...”

“TOMATO! You’re not even
a vegetable!” protested Potato.

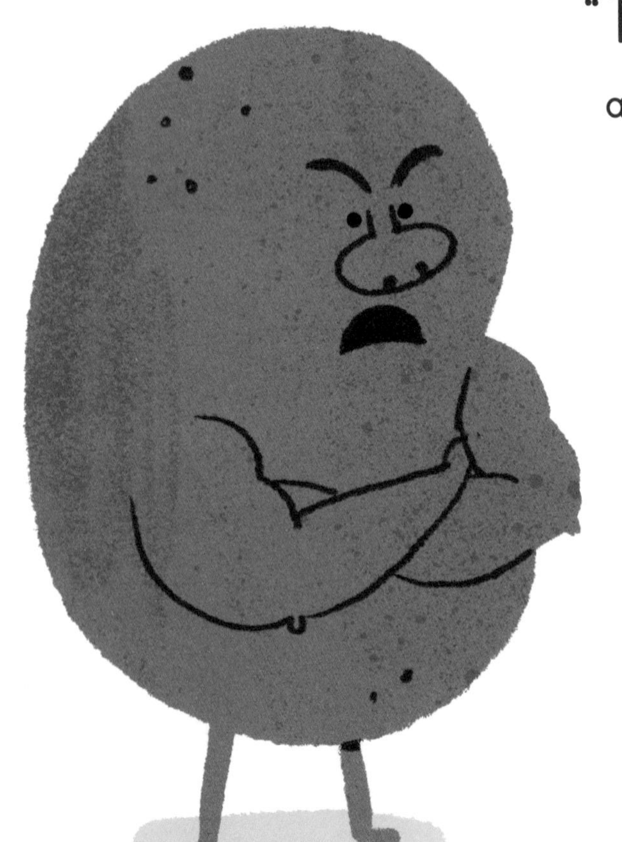

"But ME? I'm a MAGNIFICENT vegetable.
Always full of energy. After running
a marathon, I'm proud to announce,
I almost climbed to the top of
Vege-Table Mountain!"
Oh no!
So close!

"Oh!" said Broccoli. "That's where I live. You could have popped in for a cup of tea."

Everybody gasped!

Fennel fainted.

Parsnip passed out.

"You live on Vege-Table Mountain? The one by Super Stinky Swamp?" objected Aubergine.

"Yes!" said Broccoli. "The slope is super slippery and the grouchy bees are tricky... not to mention the trouble with Mrs Plum's cat. But I don't mind any of those things really."

There was silence. And then, starting with Carrot, one by one, all the vegetables began to chant: “Broccoli, Broccoli, the finest vegetable you’ll ever see!”

Broccoli blushed.

But as she accepted her award at the ceremony, she had to admit, "We vegetables are all pretty special, aren't we?"

And for the first time, everybody agreed.

THE ANATOMY OF BROCCOLI

(a super-veg)